Flies hum.
Dogs growl.
Bats screech.
Coyotes howl.
Frogs croak.
Parrots squawk.
Bees buzz.
But I TALK!

Arnold L. Shapiro

Shark

Ever see
a shark
picnic
in the park?

If he offers
you a bun

run.

Roger McGough

Contents

I Speak, I Say, I Talk

Cats purr.
Lions roar.
Owls hoot.
Bears snore.
Crickets creak.
Mice squeak.
Sheep baa.
But I SPEAK!

Monkeys chatter.
Cows moo.
Ducks quack.
Doves coo.
Pigs squeal.
Horses neigh.
Chickens cluck.
But I SAY!

If You Ever

If you ever ever ever ever ever
If you ever ever ever meet a whale
You must never never never never never
You must never never never touch its tail;
For if you ever ever ever ever ever
If you ever ever ever touch its tail,
You will never never never never never
You will never never meet another whale.

Anon.

If You Should Meet a Crocodile

If you should meet a crocodile,
  Don't take a stick and poke him;
Ignore the welcome in his smile,
  Be careful not to stroke him.
For as he sleeps upon the Nile,
  He thinner gets and thinner;
But whene'er you meet a crocodile
  He's ready for his dinner.

Anon.

Tiger

I'm a tiger
Striped with fur
Don't come near
Or I might Grrr
Don't come near
Or I might growl
Don't come near
Or I might BITE!

Mary Ann Hoberman

9

Ducks' Ditty

All along the backwater,
Through the rushes tall,
Ducks are a-dabbling,
Up tails all!

Ducks' tails, drakes' tails,
Yellow feet a-quiver,
Yellow bills all out of sight
Busy in the river!

Slushy green undergrowth
Where the roach swim—
Here we keep our larder,
Cool and full and dim!

Every one for what he likes!
We like to be
Heads down, tails up,
Dabbling free!

High in the blue above
Swifts whirl and call—
We are down a-dabbling
Up tails all!

Kenneth Grahame

The Eel

I don't mind eels
Except as meals.
And the way they feels.

Ogden Nash

Hippopotamus

The hippopotamus—
how odd—
loves rolling
in the river mud.

It makes him
neither hale nor ruddy,
just lovely
hippopotamuddy.

N. M. Bodecker

Turtles

When turtles hide within their shells
There is no way of knowing
Which is front and which is back
And which way which is going.

John Travers Moore

The Elephant

When people call this beast to mind,
  They marvel more and more
At such a little tail behind
  So *large* a trunk before.

Hilaire Belloc

Way Down South

Way down South
  where bananas grow,
A grasshopper stepped
  on an elephant's toe.
The elephant said,
  with tears in his eyes,
"Pick on somebody
  your own size."

Anon.

Whisky Frisky

Whisky frisky,
Hipperty hop,
Up he goes
To the tree top!

Whirly, twirly,
Round and round,
Down he scampers
To the ground.

Furly, curly,
What a tail,
Tall as a feather,
Broad as a sail.

Where's his supper?
In the shell.
Snappy, cracky,
Out it fell.

Anon.

16

To a Squirrel at Kyle-Na-No

Come play with me;
Why should you run
Through the shaking tree
As though I'd a gun
To strike you dead?
When all I would do
Is to scratch your head
And let you go.

W. B. Yeats

Bears

Roly poly polar bears,
Rolling in the snow,
Sliding over icebergs,
In the sea they go:

Splish, splash polar bears,
Splish, splash, splosh!

Growly brown mountain bears,
Climbing on all fours,
Hugging each other
With their big brown paws:

Stump, stomp brown bears,
Stump, stomp, stamp!

Celia Warren

Honey Bear

There was a big bear
Who lived in a cave;
His greatest love
Was honey.
He had twopence a week
Which he never could save,
So he never had
Any money.
I bought him a money box
Red and round,
In which to put
His money.
He saved and saved
Till he got a pound,
   Then spent it all
   On honey.

Elizabeth Lang

Geraldine Giraffe

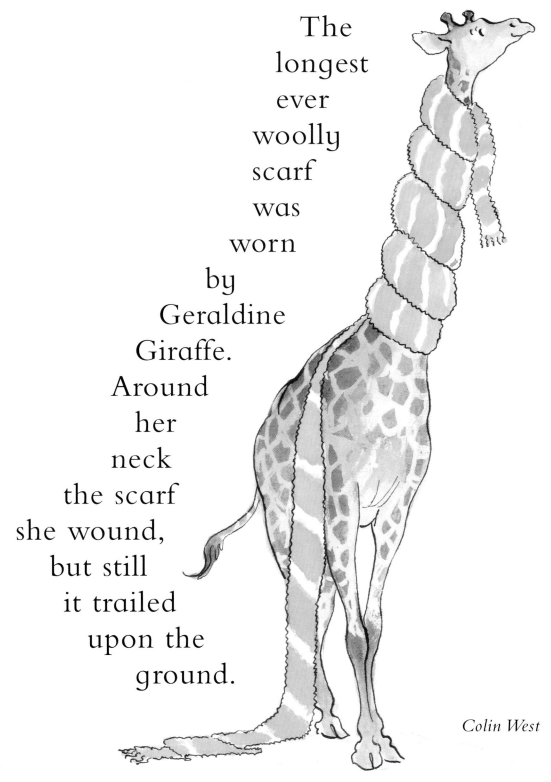

The
longest
ever
woolly
scarf
was
worn
by
Geraldine
Giraffe.
Around
her
neck
the scarf
she wound,
but still
it trailed
upon the
ground.

Colin West

Giraffes Don't Huff

Giraffes don't huff
  or hoot or howl
They never grump,
  they never growl
They never roar,
  they never riot,
They eat green leaves
And just keep quiet.

Karla Kuskin

The Kangaroo

Old Jumpety-Bumpety-Hop-and-Go-One
Was lying asleep on his side in the sun.
This old kangaroo, he was whisking
   the flies
(With his long glossy tail) from his ears
   and his eyes.
Jumpety-Bumpety-Hop-and-Go-One
Was lying asleep on his side in the sun,
Jumpety-Bumpety-Hop!

Anon.

Penguin

Big flapper
Belly tapper
Big splasher
Fish catcher
Beak snapper.

Rebecca Clark (aged 8)

The Lion and the Unicorn

The Lion and the Unicorn
  Were fighting for the crown;
The Lion beat the Unicorn
  All about the town.
Some gave them white bread,
  And some gave them brown,
Some gave them plum cake,
  And sent them out of town.

Anon.

Dinosauristory

Hocus, pocus,
plodding through the swamp;
I'm a diplodocus,
chomp, chomp, chomp!
Grass for breakfast,
I could eat a tree!
Grass for lunch and dinner
and grass for tea.
I'm a diplodocus
plodding through the swamp,
hocus-rocus pocus,
chomp, chomp, chomp!

Judith Nicholls

Five Little Owls

Five little owls in an old elm-tree,
Fluffy and puffy as owls could be,
Blinking and winking with big round eyes
At the big round moon that hung
 in the skies:
As I passed beneath, I could hear one say,
"There'll be mouse for supper, there will,
 to-day!"
Then all of them hooted, "Tu-whit, Tu-whoo!
Yes, mouse for supper, Hoo hoo, Hoo hoo!"

Anon.

The Caterpillar

Brown and furry
Caterpillar in a hurry,
Take your walk
To the shady leaf, or stalk,
Or what not,
Which may be the chosen spot.
No toad spy you,
Hovering bird of prey pass by you;
Spin and die,
To live again a butterfly.

Christina Rossetti

Little Fish

The tiny fish enjoy themselves
in the sea.
Quick little splinters of life,
their little lives are fun to them
in the sea.

D. H. Lawrence

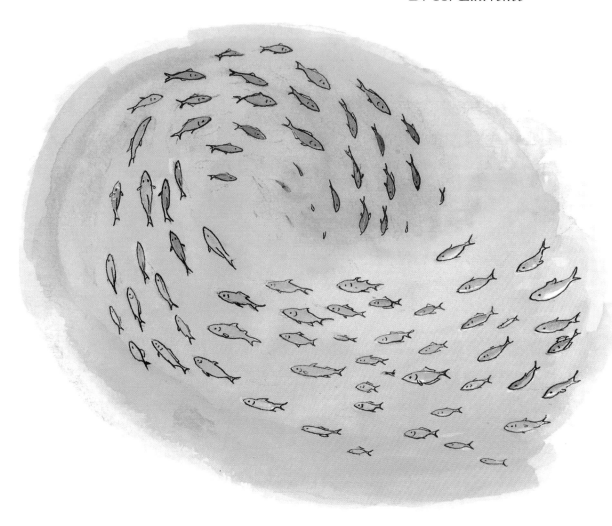

Only My Opinion

Is a caterpillar ticklish?
Well, it's always my belief
That he giggles, as he wiggles
Across a hairy leaf.

Monica Shannon

Froggie, Froggie

Froggie, froggie.
Hoppity-hop!
When you get to the sea
You do not stop.
Plop!

Anon.

Littlemouse

Light of day going,
Harvest moon glowing,
People beginning to snore,
Tawny owl calling,
Dead of night falling,
Littlemouse opening her door.

Scrabbling and tripping,
Sliding and slipping,
Over the ruts of the plough,
Under the field gate,
Mustn't arrive late,
Littlemouse hurrying now.

Into a clearing,
All the birds cheering,
Woodpecker blowing a horn,
Nightingale fluting,
Blackbird toot-tooting,
Littlemouse dancing till dawn.

Soon comes the morning,
No time for yawning,
Home again Littlemouse creeps,
Over the furrow,
Back to her burrow,
Into bed. Littlemouse sleeps.

Richard Edwards